THE TRAIN

The train

BO VICKERY

Bo Vickery

Contents

Chapter 1

Train Wagon 1

The train continued in a sedate cadence. The handles connecting the train cars made a clanging sound. Lander was still panting from his sprint to catch the train. That this had to happen to him. Working on Christmas Eve. Having to leave his family and friends, now sitting around a crackling fire, drinking an aperitif. The sandwich he had bought quickly at the station almost cost him his train. Being led by gluttony never ends well. His boss wouldn't be amused if he were too late. And what is the use of taking leave to be home for Christmas when you're called in for the smallest of trifles involving some computers? Bet it was something trivial?

He installed himself on the train bench that had seen better days. The red velour with stripes had faded. There was a loose thread in the middle of the cushion on which he sat.

He sat alone in first class in a carriage that probably dated from the sixties. Or was it the fifties? He never expected to have to take a train in this godforsaken farm town. An annual tradition, his family rented a cottage in the Ardennes. For years, they had been spending time there. But never before did he have to take a train here.

The wagon creaked and squeaked. The train track had also had better days. The inner door slid open with difficulty.

An older man stepped into the carriage and sat down two benches away. Briefcase on the bench. Impeccable suit. Hair combed tightly back. Lander guessed this man was not the type to be the funniest at home. The train rocked tremendously. It drove on with a big bang. The changing of the tracks did not run smoothly. Lander looked through the partially hazy train window. They were now on a single train track. Strange, you would think that a train line towards Brussels would run on larger, double tracks. But no, first they had to pass through a neglected single track. Wallonia remained a curious, under-developed region in Belgium.

The older man with the briefcase looked as surprised as he did outside. The man stood up, still barely holding on to his feet to keep from falling due to the train's jolting.

'Sir, excuse me, can I ask you something? Do you know why we are on this track?'

'No, I have no idea either. It's my first time taking this train, so which way or which track it takes, I don't know. I'm going to visit my grandchildren with my family. It's Christmas, after all.”

“Well, I often take this train, and this is not normal. Hopefully, the train conductor will come by soon because I want to know what is going on here.'

The older man put his glasses a little straighter on his nose. He shuffled down the aisle back to his seat. This track was not in really good shape. That much was clear. You had to do a balancing act to walk without a problem.

That was what the girl was trying to do as she struggled through the entrance door of the carriage. Long brown hair, a striking look, short-skirted. The moment Lander considered getting up to help her anyway, she opened the door. She looked a little heated and excited. She quickly sat down on the first seat she saw.

It got crowded because a young guy came in. Baggy jeans, hoodie, blue sneakers, backpack. He sat down right across from the girl. She shuffled uncomfortably back and forth. Is it okay if I sit here?' She got up and came over to Lander.

'Huh, no, please do.'

'Thanks, you know, that guy over there with his hoodie was looking at me so weirdly in the last carriage. He was spying on me, so I came over here, but he's been stalking me. So I feel safer being in the company of someone else.'

'I understand, no problem, tell me a little about yourself. That will take your mind off things.'

Before the girl could say anything, the wagon door was flung wide open by a man who looked like a biker. Long coat, leather pants, cowboy boots.

The train stopped abruptly. The biker landed on the lap of the older man with the briefcase. The girl had been thrown against Lander by the sudden stop. Lander rubbed his sore jaw. From the corner of his eye he saw the boy with the hoodie lying in the aisle, groping his knee. What made this train stop so suddenly?

Everyone crawled upright.

'I'd like to know what's happening here,' the biker hummed.

'You're not alone. Communication is not the NMBS' strongest.' 'I'm going to look for the train conductor.' The older man agreed wholeheartedly with the motorcyclist.

Even before the older man could stand up, the train conductor came in. He was also surprised by what had happened judging from the large gash through his eyebrow.

'Don't worry. There is too much snow on this track. The train driver will clear the track, and then we go to Brussels. I apologize for the delay.'

'By the way, why are we on this track?' The older man wanted to know everything.

'Something about a stationary train on the usual track. By diverting, we may take longer, but we'll get to Brussels faster than when we had to wait for that other train to get moving again.'

'It's always something with these railroads! It's already the umpteenth time that I have been delayed. It's not normal anymore. Delays are the rule and being on time is the exception.' The older man with the briefcase no longer seemed so calm because of his tirade. You would think that someone a little older would be more relaxed, but his reaction did not show it.

'I'm sorry about that, sir. We are doing everything possible to get the passengers to their destinations on time smoothly.'

The train conductor retraced his steps. He pulled at the door but could not get it open. No matter how he poked, pushed, and pulled, the door was unyielding. 'How is that possible?'

The motorcyclist stood up confidently. 'Let me.' But he, too, could not get the door open.

'It looks like this door is blocked by something.'

The older man, too, now began to pull at the door. But nothing worked.

The girl whispered to Lander, 'I think we'll be here for a while. Are you still interested in my story?'

'Yes, I'm afraid we will be here for a while.'

The girl screamed. The light of the wagon had gone out. Not a gift on such a dark day in the middle of winter. The heating or ventilation of the train car will probably stop working too, Lander thought.

A crackle sounded from the intercom in the wagon. A monotone male voice echoed.

'Hello, all. At last, we have been able to bring you together. Enjoy this ride.'

'Bringing us together, what's the point of this?' The 'briefcase man' looked nothing like the structured, calm man who had boarded this train.

'Who are you? The train conductor sounded angry.

'That will become clear to you.'

'Sir, I don't know what game you're trying to play here. This is unacceptable. Unlock that door immediately; I still have to inform the rest of the passengers.' The train conductor was now red-faced. A trickle of sweat ran down his cheek. For now it was still warm in the old train car which was not yet heated with modern air conditioning technology. It was too hot in there.

'The other passengers are already on a bus and have already been evacuated.'

'But, but, how is that possible? 'You're joking. That's impossible. 'The train driver will end this joke,' roared the train conductor.

'The driver, I'm afraid, has had a little accident. He's asleep now. It will probably be a while before he wakes up.'

'But what do you want? The girl called out to the intercom. First, there was the boy with the hoodie for whom she had fled, and now she was stuck in this carriage. For what purpose? Why?

'I want you to take this time to think hard. Think about your actions. All seven of you. I will be back in an hour to hear if you have realized why you are stuck here. All of you have had something to do with it. All of you are guilty!'

The crackle of the intercom stopped. The Voice had disappeared.

'What does he mean by that? Anyone has an idea?' It was the first time the hooded boy had opened his mouth.

'No, I can understand that you would have mishandled something, but not me, right? What would I be guilty of?' The older man looked disdainfully at the boy.

Stop it you two, this won't solve anything.' The biker tried to soothe. He had straightened up and stood strategically between the ruffians.

'I'll contact the switchboard; this can't go on like this.' The train conductor took his service cell phone. He removed himself for a moment.

'You see, this situation will be solved in no time.' The motorcyclist was firmly convinced that this was a temporary situation.

'Have I got an adventure to tell at work. At least when I get there, they'll already be starting to get impatient,' Lander chuckled.

This can't be right!' The train conductor stepped back in their direction firmly: 'I can't get a connection. The line is dead.'

Lander took out his cell phone; he, too, had no connection to the telecom network. Just like the others. Not a single cell phone had service.

'Okay, no connection, that was to be expected in this godforsaken hole, nobody can call, now what?' The older man looked around in despair.

'We can smash the windows; there are usually those little hammers in every train car anyway,' the girl said.

'Right, I should have thought of that.' The train conductor went to where usually the hammers were placed, but the holder was empty. He rushed to the next place on the other side: also empty. 'No, no, no, everything is empty.'

The calmness that had once been in the train conductor's body was instantly gone as if it had never existed.

The boy with the hoodie began banging the door. 'Hey, let us out! Is anyone in there?

'That won't do any good,' the old man sank dejectedly.

'I'm not going to let this happen,' the biker took a run at the other access door on the other side of the wagon to bang his shoulder against it. The door did not budge. The only effect was the man falling to the floor, groaning in pain.

'Strong material, those old NMBS carriages ,' Lander muttered.

'Well, those K carriages are solidly made.'

You might notice that this train was standing still for a long time.

They were in an awkward situation, but Lander was an optimist. Whatever was going on, it would get resolved. There were six of them. Both the train and themselves would be missed. Aren't all trains tracked from a signal box these days?

There was another crackle on the intercom. 'I said you had an hour to think about your actions. Not to try to escape. I assure you: you will not succeed anyway. And for those who think you will be missed: the NMBS thinks that this train is just having a defect and that the driver will solve it. If they do decide to come and remove the train, they won't get through: there happen to be a few tree trunks in the way, and the snow is blocking the tracks. Snowblowers are convenient things sometimes. You didn't think I would stop the train in a place where help can arrive immediately, did you? Besides, it's Christmas Eve: more staff are absent than present. No, you are completely at my mercy.'

'Who are you? At least have the guts to tell us who you are!' The train conductor was out of his mind with anger. He clenched his fists. His blond hair that showed from under his cap was wet with sweat. Once again, Lander saw beads of sweat making their way down his neck, like a river making its way down the valley.

'Who I am, you will hear later, but first, you must do what I ask of you: think carefully about your lives and deeds. You have only half an hour left, and then I want an answer from you.'

'Thinking about our lives and our deeds, what does that mean?' The boy ran by all the windows and felt around the edges everywhere, perhaps thinking he would find a hole or weak spot somewhere to escape anyway.

The motorcyclist paced back and forth down the aisle.

The older man had been staring in front of him for minutes as if he had been turned into a wax statue: motionless and yet fragile. The train conductor knocked on the door in a monotonous rhythm. As if that would help them.

And the girl? The girl looked defeated. Lander offered her a handkerchief as a tear welled up in her left eye. She looked cool. One of those chicks who was popular on social media, had a group of friends she often went out with but was less superficial than you would assume at first glance. That's what Lander thought when he saw her sitting there.

Each person reacts differently when under extreme stress.

There had to be a way out, but doing what everyone else was doing wouldn't get them anywhere. Lander didn't know what would happen if they didn't come up with something after half an hour,. The man sounded rather menacing through the intercom. They were locked in here for a reason.

What would happen if they did cooperate with him?

They had to try to gain time because the NMBS, the Belgian railroad company, and the emergency services would need time to free them.

Lander tried to recall the words of The Voice on the intercom. The Voice was not familiar to him. The man had spoken of a bond between everyone. So there had to be a joint event or person that connected everyone here. The man from The Voice knew what, but they did not. So the question was, who or what did they have in common?

Did the man say anything else that could be important? Lander racked his brain. Focusing was not so easy at the moment. The pounding of the train conductor on the door and the reverberation of the motorcyclist's heavy boots on the train floor didn't help much.

Focus, Lander, focus! Something else the man had said was important.

Like a bolt of lightning, the thought he was looking for a shot into his head. The man had spoken of seven people, but there were only six of them! Was this a mistake, or was there more to it? Was there a seventh person involved in this hostage situation? Lander stood up and took a good look around. He didn't see anyone he had overlooked: the train conductor, the girl, the boy with the hoodie, the older man with the briefcase, and the motorcyclist and himself: that was six. Why was The Voice talking about seven people on the intercom?

'Hey people, if we want to get through this properly, we'd better do what The Voice asks: think about our lives. What are you going to say when he contacts us again? But I noticed something else: he talked about seven people, and there are only six of us. Do any of you know why he talked about seven?'

The others had all gone silent at Lander's words.

'Seven? Wouldn't it just be a mistake?' the motorcyclist hummed.

'I don't know.' Lander sensed something was wrong.

'I don't know your name, but I think you're right. Maybe we should just do as asked.' The girl wanted to know his name.

'My name is Lander, and you?'

'Karolien.'

'Nice name.'

Meanwhile, the motorcyclist was again pacing back and forth in the wagon, but this time he was looking for something. People, over here, there is a suitcase on the rack. Does this belong to any of you?'

'No, anyone else owns the suitcase?' The boy with the hoodie was also interested in the suitcase: Come on, let's break it open, then.' He rolled up his sleeves.

'Wait, should you? Suppose there is something like a bomb inside?' The train conductor was worried.

'A bomb? Where did you get that idea?' The boy shook his head disdainfully: 'this isn't an action movie.'

'You never know with these weirdos.' The train conductor shrugged.

'What do we do: do we open the suitcase or not?' The boy had his his hands on the lock.

'Hmm, I think we'd better leave that suitcase closed. For now anyway.' The biker was not so sure of himself anymore.

'Then we would better concentrate on what we will tell The Voice when he contacts us again. And that's in about ...' Lander looked at his watch: 'fifteen minutes.'

Everyone returned to their seats in deep thought.

The suitcase intrigued Lander. It wasn't lying there by accident. But first, he had to think a little about what he would tell The Voice.

'Hello everyone, it has taken a while, but you have done what I asked, haven't you? First, who wants to tell me what he has found in his life that might explain why he ended up in this situation?

There was a deafening silence. 'If you people want to get out of this, someone will have to speak up.'

'Uh, I'll start then.' Lander had decided to bite into the sour apple. He'd much rather have been at work now, even if it was something trivial.

'I don't know exactly what you want to hear, but if the intention is to reflect on something I did wrong in my life, I can tell you something. Once, in the youth movement, when we were at camp, I stole something from a store in the village where we were staying.'

'That was it, then?'

'Yes, but not if you want me to say that I may have offended and hurt someone at times by saying and doing things, but that was not on purpose. We all hurt people unknowingly sometimes, don't we?'

'If that's all you can say, you'll have to think a little deeper, Lander; you've got a lot more to answer for!'

Lander stood perplexed. Because The Voice knew his name and especially because, according to The Voice, he had done many more wrong. He had no idea what The Voice was talking about.

'Who's next?'

'I'll lead by example.' The older man was alert again and stood up.

'My name is Wilfried Vandegenachte. I have done several things that I am not proud of: cheated on my wife, stabbed a colleague figuratively in the back to get a promotion, and often took my problems at work out on my wife and children.'

'My dear Wilfried, do you think this is what I want to hear? You may have humped as many tramps as you like, but that doesn't interest me. Nor do your scheming and family problems affect me. What you have done is unforgivable, and you don't even mention it here? How is that possible?' The Voice on the intercom was angry.

This was not going well.

Lander didn't understand; both of them had told things they knew were wrong, and still, The Voice wasn't satisfied.

What did The Voice in the intercom want from them?

"Next! 'Next, next, next, next!' the Voice now sounded very loud and impatient. But no one took the floor.

The girl quickly took the floor, for it was clear that The Voice in the intercom had lost all patience.

'I am Karolien, and I have done some things wrong. I daubed the walls at home when I was a toddler; sometimes, I sneakily pinched my little brother's arm when no one was looking, I stole candy from the store when my mom wasn't looking, I occasionally lied about where I had been, and I hurt my best friend by making remarks about her appearance. And yes, I may have posted comments on social media that I shouldn't have posted, but I did anyway, out of spite.'

'No, no, you too don't know where you really messed up. Do you think that coloring on walls with crayons is what I'm looking for! What is it with you all? Do you not know what you are doing anymore!'

Karolien sat down trembling. She rubbed her hands together convulsively and sat huddled up, staring at the ground.

Meanwhile, the Voice continued to rave: 'Do you think you will get away with this? I'm giving you one more chance!

The biker raised his voice: 'Hey, Voice or what should we call you? It would be polite of you to tell us your name too. I am Bertrand, a motorcycle fanatic. The list of what I have done wrong is not too long and not as short as I would like. If you told us what you want and what you are looking for, we would be getting somewhere. I'm happy to admit what I did wrong and apologize, but maybe I don't know what I did wrong, don't realize it, or can't think of it right now. So give us a little more explanation of what you want from us. Because we're not getting anywhere this way.'

It remained ominously silent on the intercom.

Everyone looked with concern at the motorcyclist. Had he said too much? Had he made The Voice even angrier than it already was?

Lander feared they were dealing with one of those psychopathic lunatics, in which case you never know what they're up to.

'Ah, you want a clue to know what I'm talking about. You have hurt someone very dear to me. Maybe I should give you an incentive to think better. But first, open the suitcase you see on the rack. That may well help you to better remember.'

The creaking stopped. The Voice was gone.

The motorcyclist laboriously took the suitcase from the wall rack. 'This is one heavy case. I guess it's not a bomb, is it?'

'No, I don't think so; otherwise, he wouldn't have asked to open the suitcase as an incentive. We'll all go down if it's a bomb, and then his fun will be over, and when The Voice is indeed a psychopath, it likes to play with its victims more than it likes to kill them. Death is also part of his fun, but it's foreplay, if I may call it that. That's where he gets his excitement from.'

'Where do you get all that? The boy asked suspiciously.

'Oh well, watched a lot of detective series. You learn a thing or two from that.'

The suitcase lay on an empty seat.

'Everyone ready? The biker carefully pressed the two buttons to open the briefcase.

The lid popped open.

The motorcyclist jumped back and vomited behind a seat.

The boy with the hoodie looked at the trunk curiously and was seemingly calm.

Lander stepped cautiously closer.

A stinky smoke filled the wagon.

Lander looked inside the suitcase: there was a corpse inside.

The corpse of a woman.

The boy wanted to shut the trunk's lid quickly, but Lander stopped him and bent over the trunk with a handkerchief in front of his mouth. He promptly took out the passport that stuck out from the suitcase's side pocket, as well as well as the sheet of paper above the woman. Then he signaled the boy to close the suitcase lid. The boy tried to pick up the suitcase to place it further away, but he was unsuccessful. The trunk weighed too much.

The motorcyclist, who by now had somewhat recovered from what he had seen, took a firm hold of the trunk and placed it as far as he could. Lander tried to slide open one of the windows above the train windows to ventilate the carriage to remove the pungent stench. In a vain attempt to stop the smell, the older man sat with a handkerchief in front of his nose, as did the train conductor. The girl, Karolien, was gagging. Wilfried, the older man, had returned to his lethargy and seemed locked in his cocoon.

With great difficulty Lander got one window slightly open, a tiny chink. He couldn't get the other windows any looser.

As if they were secured. So they were in danger.

Lander slowly felt a sense of panic creeping up on him. No, he had to stay calm. Panic wouldn't help anyone.. There had to be a way to escape from this.

Karolien was crying silently. 'Hey, everything will be okay, just believe me now. We'll get out of this.' Karolien laid her head on Lander's shoulder.

'Who was that in the suitcase?' Lander was brought back to reality by the train conductor.

He took the passport from the suitcase out of his coat pocket. He flipped it open: 'Leen Janssens. Does this name mean anything to any of you?'

No one responded. Then there was the sheet of paper. What did it say?

'I am number one.'

'No, we will be killed. You see, it's a psychopath.' Karolien was even more in a panic.

'That doesn't bode well.' The motorcyclist shook his head.

'Shouldn't we investigate what the connection is between us all? According to The Voice, we somehow have a connection, and that's why we're here. I want to get out of here, so come on, say it.' The boy in the hoodie didn't feel like staying there any longer either. 'I live in Beveren, dropped out of school, unemployed. Gaming is my thing. I have two brothers and a sister. Does anyone have any idea what your connection to me might be?'

'Well, you could start by telling me your name.' The biker's dry remark hit home.

Meanwhile, he walked around, feeling all the rods, seats, and tables to see if anything was loose. He unsuccessfully tried again to pull down a window with all his might. 'Damn, there's nothing loose here to smash a window with or pry open a door.' The motorcyclist stomped his foot against a table again, but it didn't budge.

Yes, everything was still solidly made in the old days,' sighed the old man.

The boy continued: 'Xavier Beernaert is my name, does that ring a bell to anyone?'

'No, not really.' The biker shrugged.

Lander racked his brain, but he couldn't think of anything that would bring him to remember the boy.

Karolien hesitantly asked Xavier, 'Do you sometimes go out at The Miracle Club?'

'Of course, who doesn't?'

'Yes, now we're getting somewhere.' The biker complemented, 'I sometimes work as a bouncer at The Miracle Club.'

But before they could exchange any more information, The Voice echoed back, 'Have you found my surprise yet?'

Everyone was silent, the air heavy with the silence that weighed like lead on everyone.

'No one has anything to say? If you were still wondering: that was the first of seven. Now there are still six of you. The only question is how much longer?'

Lander shifted uncomfortably in his seat. There had to be a way to silence this voice and escape from this situation.

'Have you found a connection between you yet? Come on, who's going to speak up?'

'The Miracle Club,' growled the biker.

'Bravo, you have found the connection between you all. The Miracle Club, that's what brought you to me. But I think you still don't quite know why you're here. I'll give you another fifteen minutes to figure that out, too. One person will have to leave after that.'

The Voice left everyone hushed. 'Someone is leaving? Is he going to kill one of us? Fear resonated in Karolien's voice and made her sound thinner.

'Rest assured, he won't hurt you,' the biker soothed. 'I won't let that happen. He'll have to deal with me.'

'What are you going to do? The older man had returned to the realm of the living. 'We're all going to get killed, but first, he'll play with us. He's wrong, by the way: I've never been to The Miracle Club. I don't even know where that is?'

'You don't know The Miracle Club? Then that Voice is wrong. He's just bullying us like that!' The boy shouted indignantly in the intercom direction as if this would help The Voice hear him better.

'The Miracle Club is a club where music is played, and people go dancing. Doesn't that tell you anything, Wilfried?' Lander had sat down next to him. The older man shook his head denyingly.

Curious. The Voice was not infallible after all. Or was the older man's memory failing? Or did he not want to tell what was his connection to the The Miracle Club? For years, there had been rumors that the club was involved in drug trafficking and other unsavory practices.

'We have to look for the why. If The Voice believes that The Miracle Club connects us, something must have happened there that is important to him.'

'But unimportant to us, or we would know it immediately. Whereas to God, I don't know.' The older man shook his head in utter confusion, his hair by now wet with sweat at the bottom; even though it was freezing cold outside, the air conditioning in the train car was off and getting cold.

Anxiety sweat you get at all temperatures.

'As a bouncer, I did experience some things at The Miracle Club, but whatever I experienced, I don't think there was any- thing so wrong as to justify a hostage situation like this. So sorry, but I don't know.

The boy added, "I went out there a lot, but I'm as innocent as a lamb. However, the boy's grin suggested the opposite of what he said.

Yeah, yeah, I don't buy it..' Karolien reacted fiercely: 'The way you were staring at me funny just now.... You are a creep. I wouldn't be surprised if you were harassing girls. Creep!'

'Calm down, calm down, boring fury. I can't help when girls come at me like bees at honey. It's out of my hands.' The boy made an innocent face, but that made him more suspicious.

'I've already seen you at work over there, all but innocent. Admit it: you molested, assaulted, raped, or worse, someone there!' Karolien called out loudly as if she wanted to make sure The Voice could hear her.

'Hey, say, stay calm. First, tell me what you have to do with The Miracle Club? Hey, maybe you're not so innocent either!'

'I go out at The Miracle Club once in a while, but that's it.'

'Old man, you say you have nothing to do with The Miracle Club and don't even know about it, but that's impossible. Think again!

'But no, lad, Xavier, I have nothing to do with The Miracle Club, I tell you!'

'Are you sure you're not developing dementia?' Before the boy could say anything else, the older man's hand left an imprint on the boy's face. 'Ouch, what's that for?'

'That's for the lack of respect towards your elder. Call it my gift.' The older man had regained all his strength.

'We won't get anywhere like this,' sighed the biker.

'Just to recap,' Lander decided to take the lead before some in the train car were already finishing each other off. 'Karolien used to out at The Miracle Club, so did Xavier, and Bertrand was a bouncer there.'

'What were you?'

'I don't know. I've been out there, but not that often either. Rather rarely. So I'll be honest: I don't know how I am involved with anything that happened at The Miracle Club either.'

'Fine, another denier. We're not getting anywhere this way.' The boy raised his hands in the air.

'I'm not a denier,' Lander growled, I went out there, but not often. And I don't remember anything special ever happening.'

'And you? The boy turned to the train conductor.

'Me - what would I have to do with some nightclub or disco? I don't go there, why should I? I'm a family man.'

'You wouldn't want to know how many family men let themselves go when they're out and about,' the biker hummed.

'I don't.'

'Then The Voice is wrong, or you are lying to us,' said the boy.

'Ah boy, I'm not like you,' sneered the train conductor as he pushed the boy aside hard-handedly. The train conductor fell down on a seat.

At that precise moment, The Voice echoed: Have you found out anything new or not?'

The old man spoke up: 'We think it has something to do with an event at The Miracle Club, but we don't know exactly what.'

'You folks disappoint me. You'd think people would know what they were doing, know what disastrous choices they've made, what their choices result in. But no. You are as irresponsible and shallow as most people. You don't even know what you have done. Well, I will tell you so that you will know and understand what will happen here is solely due to yourself'.

The Voice sounded angry.

That did not bode well. It remained silent for a moment.

'Does the name Antje Goetschalckx mean anything to any of you? Perhaps not.'

The Voice waited.

No one responded; everyone continued to stare ahead.

Lander looked curiously at the others.

Karolien looked at her feet.

The boy shrugged, the older man shook his head, and the train conductor looked outside.

The motorcyclist paced. Lander didn't get the impression that anyone knew anything. The name didn't ring a bell to him either.

The voice continued its explanation, 'Of course, you don't know who Antje was. One little article in the paper, "Girl, commits suicide after a night out at The Miracle Club." Somewhere in the corner of the paper, there was much more spectacular news that day.'

You could hear the frustration in The Voice. 'But she deserved better. Antje deserved much better than a small corner in the newspaper. Antje deserved to be alive. To laugh, to drink, to party. Only now, she can't. She can no longer because of you!

'Us? The biker shouted the word. 'Now you listen carefully: we, yes, we have nothing to do with what happened to your tenderly beloved Antje!'

'Oh really? I'll tell you what you have to do with it. If you believe you have nothing to do with it, I'll refresh your memory. At least if you have a memory!' The Voice cleared his throat. 'It was May 1, 2017. Antje went out to The Miracle Club to celebrate her new vacation job. But someone gave her GHB. Possibly put it in her drink without her knowing. So she didn't know what she was doing anymore. She had lost all control. She didn't feel well. She wanted to go home. Be safe. So she left The Miracle Club. She felt miserable. She asked the bouncer for help. But he laughed her question away. He thought she was just another drunk slut looking for attention. He sent her away in no unclear words. And guess who that bouncer was?'

'Euhm, yes, It could have been me, but I don't remember. It does happen from time to time that I send a girl away.' The biker thought about what he just heard. He looked startled.

Lander shuffled on his seat. Suppose The Voice was right that they all had something to do with Antje's suicide. Lander racked his brain, but her name didn't ring a bell no matter how hard he tried.

Maybe a picture would help, but they didn't have one.

'Hey, look, I'm sorry about what happened to that girl and that I didn't believe her and therefore didn't help her. But how could I have known that she was drugged instead of just another drunken attention seeker but drugged?'

'Excuses, weak excuses, do you know the motto that you should help a person in need? Motto, it's not even a motto. It's in the criminal code: you are obliged to help people in need . Why didn't you help her?'

'I don't know ... '

The motorcyclist suddenly seemed much smaller than he was. As if The Voice's words had made him shrink. 'That's just the thing about sexy girls. They're so confusing. She must have looked drunk and acted weird. Otherwise, I really wouldn't have sent her away. I'm not a heartless bouncer. You have to believe me.'

'You have a hand in her death.'

'But no, how could I have known she would kill herself?' The biker said indignantly.

'Suicide, it wasn't suicide! That's what the newspaper made of it, that's what the prosecution made of it: dissolute girl takes GHB, goes outside, goes to the water, and jumps in.'

'I didn't kill her, did I?'

'You made a choice not to help her. You are complicit in her suicide, if I can put it that way. If you had helped her, called a doctor, brought her back inside, and found someone to take her home, Antje would still be alive. Because of your choice, she jumped into the water under the influence.'

'Sorry, man, that was not my intention.' The biker looked pleadingly at the intercom as if it were a living being.

'Do you think something like that is just forgivable? Do you think that? Yes, I forgive, as you saw in that suitcase. She, Leen Janssens, also apologized for what she had done. So I forgave her and gave her eternal peace. That way, she didn't have to feel guilty for the rest of her life. It is an act of mercy that I perform. In the same way, you will also receive eternal rest, but not yet. First, I have to talk to the others again.'

The motorcyclist had sat down in bewilderment. How could he have gotten into this situation? He who had always dutifully done his job as a bouncer. Yes, he had occasionally refused to allow some bimbo or drunk guest to enter or ignored their ramblings. But since when does not listening to the nonsense of drunken youngsters or youngsters under the influence lead to your death sentence, years later? The motorcyclist did not understand. Why did this have to happen to him?

'Who's turn is it now? Ah yes, maybe start with the wrinkled man with the briefcase first. Mr. Correctness. You were there too that night.'

The old man stood up indignantly, 'I've never been to that Miracle Club or whatever that night temple is called.'

'Hmm, then I'll refresh your memory for a moment. Remember you promised to pick up your granddaughter at a nightclub because it was her first night out and her parents had to go to some party at their service club. You were to pick her up at the corner of Stationsstraat and Baliestraat. And what nightclub is located there in the Baliestraat? Yes: The Miracle Club. Does that mean anything to you?

'Oh, yes, I remember now: indeed, I may have picked up my granddaughter there, but that has only happened three times.'

'Do you remember a girl asking you for help on one of those occasions? Tapped on your window? No?

'Yes, a girl may have tapped on my window, but the place is full of those drugged-up sluts drawn to a fancy car like bees to a beehive. They just want to rip off my money for a blowjob.'

'No, that's where you're wrong: Antje desperately tapped on your window to ask for your help to get her to a hospital, but what did you do? Nothing. Just nothing. Staring straight ahead and making a waving gesture. A person in need you abandon, Mr. Correct. That doesn't square with the wrinkle-free image you're so fond of cultivating, does it?

The older man was shocked. He would never abandon someone in need of help. Had he become so superficial that he looked at the world from an ivory tower? Doubt struck. His self-image had just been shattered and lay on the ground like a broken mirror.

'And now, let's look at the train conductor. Conductor or wait, these days this is called train steward. So guiding a train is the only thing you can do, guide the train, not the passengers. At least judging by the way you treated Antje. Let's go back in time. To the time when you worked as a bartender in The White Bear, a locak pub. Does it ring any bells now?'

'No, I met so many people in The White Bear, girls, and women. How should I know if I ever saw that Antje of yours?'

'I thought so: again, one of those who is more occupied by hitting on girls at the bar than with his job. Do you do that on the train too?'

'No, I just don't know who you're talking about?'

'It was May 1, extra busy because many had the day off and had taken leave the day after, so they had a long weekend. The White Bear was packed. The atmosphere was sultry. Can you elaborate on what happened then?'

'Pff, no.' The train conductor took his cap off. A few sweaty hairs came out despite the cold. The man took a handkerchief to rub his hair for a moment.

'You needed to get out for a bit and asked your colleague if you could go for a smoke for ten minutes since you had been at the bar almost every evening. Your colleague agreed, so you went to the side door of The White Bear to have a smoke outside on the side street. You were standing there blowing smoke into the air when a girl came shuffling towards you. My Antje. She asked if you could help her. She had lost her money and her smartphone. She was feeling miserable and wanted to make a phone call home so someone could come and pick her up. Like our Wilfried here who came to pick up his granddaughter. And what do you think you were doing?'

'Nothing surely? Otherwise, I wouldn't be sitting here now.'

'Indeed, how did you guess! You did nothing. You shouted, "go away, you drugged up slut, son of a bitch." You even pushed her away, causing her to fall to the ground and hurt her knee. You only added to the misery Antje was in. No, you preferred to puff your cigarette. And then you just went back inside as if nothing was wrong. At the same time, Antje lay there on the ground and had to cling to a lamppost to stand up. You just went back in to pour pints.'

'Yeah, uh, sorry, hey. I'm sorry. I don't know what to say. I didn't know how bad it was. I swear! The train conductor shouted, looking exhausted.

'That was number three, three more to go. Is there anyone who wants to say something on their own?'

Lander looked at Karolien and the boy with the hoodie. No one was making any move to speak. Lander had to admit that the name didn't mean anything to him either. He didn't know what he would have done to get that girl killed. Antje, Antje, the name drew a blank in his head.

'Let's talk about Xavier. Xavier Beernaert'.

The Voice pronounced Beernaert very slowly and with emphasis on the first syllable. 'You're a tough guy, aren't you. That's how you think of yourself anyway, if I'm not mistaken, with your cool tattoos. With that hoodie on your head, you consider yourself tough. But in reality, you're just hiding. You may think the world of yourself, but you're just a retarded asshole.'

When The Voice said that, the boy jumped straight. 'Who are you to call me a retarded jackass! You consider yourself strong and significant behind your intercom, but you're just a loser, a coward who doesn't dare show his face! Putain! The boy hit the wall of the train hard with his fist. It is evident that the boy's fist was suffering more from the blow than the wall, but the boy did not move a single finger.

Anger often hides the pain and makes you numb.

'That's what despair feels like. You feel the pain, don't you? The pain of not being able to do anything. Well, that's what I felt: being unable to do anything while my Antje was so misunderstood, neglected, and ignored until the pain became too strong for her. The drugs had numbed her feelings until all she felt was confusion and pain. Now you know what it is like to feel that way. It sucks, doesn't it?'

There was a sound of laughter. The laughter of a madman.

'Yes, this sucks. Whatever I did to your Antje, I'm sorry, okay! Got it!' Xavier was angry. That was obvious. He wasn't used to being locked up like this, to not being free to do what he wanted.

'Oh, you're sorry, but you don't know what to be sorry for. That's pretty easy, isn't it? The Voice sounded harsh.

'What do you want me to say? Tell me what you want me to do? Tell me, I am completely at your disposal!' The boy stood with his arms raised as if he was surrendering completely. He stood wide-legged in the center aisle of the train car.

'Antje stumbled on down the street, towards home. You saw her walking and what did you do? You went to her....'

'That's good isn't it. I had noticed her, hadn't I?'

'Don't interrupt me!' The train car just barely thundered through the shouts of The Voice.

'Antje walked around aimlessly. You went to her and what did you do? Do you remember?

'Asking if she was all right, surely?'

'No, no, you didn't. You tried to hit on her. You asked if she felt like going with you to do a number. That's what you did! You would do a girl even if she is half unconscious from the GHB. A gir who didn't know where she was, who was miserable. That's what turns you on! How sick can you be!'

'Yes, sorry, indeed, I shouldn't have done that. I'm sorry, okay!'

Xavier waved his arms wildly as if he wanted to fight an invisible enemy.

'Who's the loser now? Me having you in my power or a guy so desperate that he hits on a drugged girl to get a shag? And what did you accomplish? You've made Antje even more miserable than she was. She ran away from you as fast as she could.

In the direction of the canal. What if she hadn't run into you? Then she might have continued walking down the street and get home safely. But what did you do? You gave someone who was down an extra kick towards the abyss!'

'I'm sorry, I already said that!'

'Tell that to Antje!'

'Well, I can't very well do that anymore. Right? Hey, she's lying on the graveyard.'

'You, you, you ... '

The intercom was turned off.

The biker stood in front of the boy and had grabbed his shoulders. 'That wasn't smart. This is a man who's psychologically unhinged you're talking to.'

'Xavier, it's really not smart to upset The Voice like this.'

'He holds our fate in their hands. Not just yours, but all of ours, so hold back a little, please.'

The old man turned to the boy: 'I know you're having a hard time. It's not easy being young nowadays. I also understand that you are angry to be here. I am too, but now we must be wise and choose self-preservation. Trying to survive because you never know what a fool like that is up to. So I hope you understand that by riling up The Voice, you are getting yourself into trouble and all of us with you. So please hold back a little. Can you do that?'

The older man looked sternly at the boy whose hoodie now lay lifeless on his back.

'Yes, I'm sorry I let myself go, but in this situation ...' The boy's voice suddenly sounded brittle. He seemed on the brink of tears.

'Come on,' the motorcyclist patted Xavier's back, 'we will discuss what we can do against The Voice.'

The motorcyclist and the boy settled into the pleasant-feeling seats with the green stripes of velour.

An old train car like this did have its charm. Standing still in the snowy landscape where you saw nothing modern, just nature, seemed like a leap back in time.

'By the way, how does he know what we do and say?' Karolien let out another laugh. 'He knows what we do. As if he can see everything. There must be cameras around here somewhere. But that's unusual in a train carriage, isn't it? And certainly not in such an old carriage. You're not generally filmed in one, am I wrong?

'No, you're right!' Lander jumped up. 'There are cameras and microphones in here somewhere, but that also means that The Voice must have had the opportunity to install all that in the train car before we got on it.'

'It's not that hard, you know.' The train conductor moved closer to join the conversation. 'No train set runs 24 hours at a time. They are cleaned after their shift and then placed on a side track. Waiting to be driven back to their place of departure the next morning. Anyone can get in at night to install a camera if they break open the doors. The Desiro train model even has cameras in it already. But in old train cars as these K carriages, of course, there are none.'

'Isn't such a carriage checked before it leaves again?' Karolien tried to understand how The Voice could have installed the cameras and microphones.

'Yes, but only the train conductor makes his rounds in all the carriages, checks that the water is okay, the toilets work, and everything is clean. He doesn't look for cameras or micro-phones. Moreover, look around: do you see any? The Voice must have been able to break into a train car without leaving any traces.'

Sometimes you feel more than you see. 'Maybe an inside job? Someone from the cleaning staff?' The motorcyclist began to look furtively on the ceiling, searching for the cameras and microphones.

He felt along the edges to ensure that his fingers would discover what his eyes didn't see.

Everyone watched with anxiety, peering around inquisitively.

'Yes, here, I've got one! You can hardly see them: so small! Come and have a look!'

You could see a tiny pinhead from which a wire was hanging.

All went to the biker to look at what was hidden.

'Now what? Karolien sighed, 'if we remove the camera, The Voice will only get angrier. He probably is watching us looking for his cameras and microphones and wanting to get rid of them. How will he react to that? Not so happy, I think: do we want to provoke him by destroying his equipment?'

'Shit, you're right. Maybe it's best just to leave everything as it is.' Even the boy had his doubts.

'On the other hand: if he can no longer follow us or eavesdrop, maybe it will be easier to escape?' Lander still assumed that there had to be a way to get off that damned train.

And that would be easier if The Voice didn't know what they were doing.

So, as expected, The Voice intervened. 'Hey! Good on you you people for finding a camera, but I'd leave where it is if I were you. Because without cameras or microphones, the fun is gone for me. I might as well kill you all right now. And you know, I'd rather play with you a little bit first. And I suspect you all want to live as long as possible.'

He would not simply allow them to put a stop to his preconceived plan.

No, Lander thought, they were the mice in this game, and The Voice was the cat who took pleasure in playing with them. Again it was silent. The Voice was quiet, as was everyone else in the wagon.

Lander heard Karolien weeping quietly. 'It's going to be all right,' he whispered in her ear.

She looked at him with a feeble smile, 'Why did I have to meet you just now, when I am going to die.'

'But you're not going to die.'

'Yes, I am. I feel it. We won't get out of here in one piece.' Tears ran down her cheeks.

Lander anxiously rubbed away some tears with his hand. Her glance made him melt away, even in this cold.

For a moment, everything seemed far away.

'We'll leave those cameras up, shall we?' The boy strolled around: 'Here's another one. Yes, at least there will be camera footage of me, even if I'm no longer alive. Always wanted to be on television.'

The boy did a moonwalk. As if he had to perform in front of an audience. He still thought it was funny. 'Anyone else has an idea how we can escape?'

'You shut up. If you hadn't tried to fondle Antje, she probably would never have been near the canal or jumped into the water. Then I wouldn't have ended up in this situation,' the old man snapped at Xavier.

'I can say the same about you: if you had offered Antje help while you were waiting in your car, I would never have run into her. Then she might not have committed suicide .'

The boy was not going to take the blame for this.

.'Bickering won't get us anywhere.' The biker wanted to keep the peace.

Lander too had his say 'That's right. We won't get anywhere accusing each other of who is to blame for allowing others to die.'

'I'm curious to know what you have on your rap sheet. You must have done something to make Antje make her fatal decision. You won't be that innocent either.'

As if The Voice had heard them, The Voice broke his silence.

'Who's next? Wait a minute, I'm being polite and I give priority to the women. In this case, Karolien. 'Karolien, Karolien, don't you remember how you treated Antje?'

'No, I don't remember, but I beg you, whatever I did, I didn't do it willingly or on purpose.'

'If you don't know what you did, it's hard to say it wasn't intentional. You don't even know what you did. All right then, I will put you out of your misery.'

'No!'

Karolien began to sob while her eyes were still red from her previous crying fit.

'Not literally. That's for later: I will put you out of your misery figuratively by telling you what your relationship is to Antje.' The Voice was silent.

Karolien humbly bowed her head.

'Antje ran away distraught after her encounter with Xavier. She fled. While running away, of course, she wasn't looking very well. She collided with another girl walking down the street with her smartphone in hand. So you can even wonder if it was Antje's fault that both ladies collided. Anyway, Antje lost her balance and fell. The other girl bent over her and pulled her upright. 'That was you, Karolien.'

'Then I haven't done anything wrong, have I?'

'Until you heard Antje speak. Because of the GHB, she talked unclearly and incoherently. She asked you for help: to take her home. But who would want to take a gibbering girl who was clearly drunk? Not you, eh Karolien? No, you scolded her and walked on because you had a date with your friends at a party. That was much more important.'

'Sorry, I didn't know someone had drugged her. I didn't know how bad it was. Otherwise, I would have helped her. You have to believe me. I'm so sorry about that! Sorry, sorry, sorry.' Karolien had fallen to her knees.

'Stop begging. It doesn't help. Everyone must take responsibility for their choices, including you: you chose not to help Antje, so now you bear the consequences.'

'But I'm sorry, how could I have known she was in such bad shape? I don't even remember the incident. I meet so many people.'

'Look, just look. You would have immediately seen that Antje was in trouble and needed urgent help. But I'm not going to discuss this any further. I will now talk about the last person who saw her alive. And that's you, Lander!'

Lander stood up straight.

He was wondering what The Voice had to tell him because he still didn't know which girl The Voice was talking about.

'Lander, the gentlemen. Except with Antje. Antje was at the bridge over the canal. Does that tell you anything?'

'No, I don't remember anything like that.'

'Antje was just leaning against the bridge railing. She was having a bad time with it. She was hallucinating, didn't know where she was. You walked past her. You looked oddly in her direction, walked on, but then turned back. And you spoke to her.'

'Yes, I am like that, and what did I say?'

'You asked if everything was okay. Antje shook her head no. But she didn't say anything. You asked again if you could help her. She shook no but said nothing else. What is it then, you asked? Antje shrugged her shoulders. She was completely absorbed in her intoxication, since she then began to laugh uncontrollably. She laughed her head off. She laughed at nothing. What did you do? You just walked away again.'

'Yes, what would you do if someone reacted like that. I thought she was a madwoman,. She was laughing at me. At least I suppose I must have thought so because, quite frankly, your story doesn't ring a bell. Are you sure you want me around?'

'Oh yes, Lander, it's you I must have. I'm sure of that. What do you have to say to this?'

'Sorry, I guess? But I really can't remember that event. If I was involved and didn't help her, I am sorry.'

'See, now you all know what your part was in Antje's death. Because let's face it: this wasn't suicide. Antje was driven to this point by what happened that night. By your actions and choices, you drove someone to her death. How does that feel?'

'Actually, you should foremost find the one who put the GHB in her drink, not us.' The train conductor resisted The Voice's conclusion.

'Yes, that's right, well said.' The older man said pugnaciously.

'No, wrong thinking. Each event was a building block that led to her death. It's not just the first step: GHB was put in her drink, but your actions also led her to death. You all had the opportunity to take her home, seek medical attention, or take care of her. But no one did anything. No, it was much easier to be occupied with yourself in your little world not considering other people: you are allequally responsible.'

'Well it's easier for you I guess, You just don't know who put the GHB in her drink, so you aim your arrows at us while we were just bystanders, no more than that. We were just being there, doing what we thought we had to do.' The train conductor made a throwaway gesture toward the intercom.

'You were more than bystanders, you are accomplices, and now I will make you feel that. This is your first assignment: determine which one of you is most responsible and who bears the greatest guilt in what happened to Antje. That person stays here. The others may go to the next wagon.'

'And what will happen to the person who stays behind?' The older man was suspicious.

But The Voice remained silent.

'How are we supposed to do that? I think everyone bears equal or no responsibility in this.' The train conductor placed his cap back correctly on his head.

'I rather wonder what will happen to those who stay behind and those who have to go to another carriage: what is the right choice?' The older man did not trust the matter.

'Should we even choose? What if we do nothing? What if we simply disobey and do nothing. What can The Voice do to us then? If we resist, all of us, then The Voice can do nothing.' The biker straightened his leather jacket.

'I don't want to choose either,' Karolien muttered.

'You know what, we just don't choose. We'll stay right where we are. Let him figure it out!' Lander was adamant.

He wasn't going to designate anyone to stay behind. 'We stick together.'

'Like the three musketeers:"One for all, all for one"'. The older man raised his hand in the air like a sword.

The intercom crackled again.

'Now I thought you were smarter than that. You don't want to choose? Okay, then it immediately ends here for everyone. However, anyone who goes to the next wagon still has a chance of getting out of here alive. Think about that carefully.'

Before anyone could even say anything the boy suddenly walked quickly to the train door to pull it open to get to the other carriage. It didn't work immediately.

Until a click was heard, after which the door opened automatically, he didn't care knocking over the suitcase.

His hood had fallen off from the effort.

The boy was gone.

He ran to the next carriage.

'That's one less chance for the others.'

The Voice had rubbed salt into the wound once more.

A scuffle ensued, pushing and pulling.

Suddenly the group feeling was gone, as everyone tried to run as fast as possible to the train door to the other wagon.

Each for himself.

Karolien fell to the ground through the narrow passage, but Lander pulled her up and dragged her into the other wagon.

Both the train conductor and the motorcyclist were already waiting.

The older man remained behind in the last carriage.

They saw that the train door was closing in front of him.

No matter how the older man pulled at it, he could not get the train door to move.

He was shouting, but they could not understand what he was saying.

They saw him screaming. Despair in his eyes.

After the section with the accordion walls, the connecting door between the two cars slowly closed automatically, hiding the older man from their view.

No one said anything.

Chapter 2

Train Wagon 2

The intercom was also present in this train car as a whistle sounded.

The whistling of a man.

As if someone was just taking a walk and whistling as they went.

Then they heard the older man.

His shouting and screaming cut through the bone.

Lander cringed.

Karolien wept.

The motorcyclist just stood there covering his ears.

The train conductor stared at his shoes.

The boy stared ahead without emotion.

It seemed it lasted for hours, but in reality, it was only minutes.

Maybe even seconds.

Time always seems to slow down when you're waiting..

Then it became silent.

The silence lasted even longer. It was cold.

The train car was not heated, and it was snowing outside.

Silence ruled outside the train car as well.

Snow always brings silence.

The Voice broke this fragile but burdened silence: "So, now you show your true faces. You leave the oldest of the group helpless. The man who just a few minutes ago convincingly shouted 'one for all, all for one. What must he have thought about you those last few minutes, what must he have felt. Look how he has been betrayed. He, who, after all, had not done so much wrong compared to some others, had to pay first, sorry second, and face my wrath. Well, well, now I know I'm right about you. Only self-interest counts. That's how it always goes with people anyway: only you count. No consideration for others. Even if, just before that, there was talk of group interest. That was quickly forgotten. In the end, it is me, me, I, and the rest can go to hell. Just like you left Antje to die. All for the freedom of the "me". Hmm, I'm going to take a moment to think about what I will do with you guys and what the next assignment will be. In the meantime, you can have another chat about your behavior. You don't have much more to do anyway.'

A knock sounded.

The biker had knocked on a window with his hand.

He began to walk back and forth hurriedly, looking whether he could see anything that might help him escape.

Whether there was anything to break the window.

But the train car looked the same as the previous one.

There was nothing that could be loosened to smash the window with.

'Why did you have to run to this carriage? The train conductor began hurling reproaches at the boy. Piece of scum. All the more since you bear most responsibility for what happened to Antje.'

'Hey, don't blame me: didn't you also run here without taking any notice of the others?' The boy defended himself.

'What else could I do?'

'You could have agreed with the rest about how we would all get out of here together without anyone being left behind. Hand in hand, for all I care?'

'Yes, why didn't you?' The train conductor was red-faced with anger.

'This isn't doing any good. We all hurried here with no regard for others. Let's all be honest about that.' Lander had no desire to argue in these tense moments.

He felt nauseous.

He had helped cause someone's death by abandoning that person.

Maybe The Voice was right, and he had also left that girl, Antje?

'What is The Voice planning to do with us now? Karolien asked the question as panic echoed in her Voice. 'We saw what he did to that poor old man, just murdered in cold blood. He must be planning to do the same to us ... ' Her voice broke.

'We won't let it come to that.' Lander embraced her.

'We've seen how you take care of others. I wouldn't trust him. You saw how he abandoned the older man. He will do the same to you.'

'Shut up! The train conductor gave the boy a shove, making him fall backward. The boy lay dizzy on the ground. A fine trickle of blood ran down his ear. The boy felt the back of his head.

'Say, have you lost it completely?'

'Ouch, my head. You wounded me! The boy looked at his bloodied hand in surprise.

The biker had a white handkerchief in his hand and walked over to the boy to hold it to the back of his head.

He examined the boy's head.

'It's not too bad, just a big cut. You may have landed badly on something. A head always bleeds a lot. Don't worry. I know what I'm talking about. Being a bouncer I had to get a Red Cross First Aid certificate. Things like that happen all the time when you work in the nightlife. Here, hold this to your head. Press hard. The bleeding will stop.'

The boy took the handkerchief from the motorcyclist.

Once the bleeding stopped, he put his hoodie back on with a face like thunder.

The train conductor did not apologize but sulkily sat down a little further, out of sight of the rest.

'The Voice needn't kill us off. We'll do it ourselves.' Lander sighed.

They would never find a way out this way.

He started to look around again to see if there was any chance of escaping. No result..

No crack, opening or open window.

They were stuck in this train car just the same.

The only thing that stood were large television screens hung up on the wall.

'I have something else for you.'

The Voice was back. 'Because I think you guys could use a little relaxation. I see tensions are getting quite high. So I have a little movie clip for you. You'll watch it on the television screens mounted on the walls here. Or wait, maybe the clip isn't so relaxing. Because it's a video of Antje? So that you can see clearly who's death you caused.'

The screens came to life.

At the same time, the subject of the clip was dead.

The screens were modern, probably newly hung, and contrasted with the shiny wood look of the train walls and the velour seats.

A movie began in which you saw a happy girl.

A girl who enjoyed life and was loved by her family.

You could see that she was popular with her friends.

The clip made Lander shuffle uncomfortably on his train seat.

Karolien and the motorcyclist were also touched.

The train conductor couldn't see Lander because his back was to them.

The boy looked as emotionless as ever.

Although the video may only have lasted fifteen minutes, it seemed like hours.

Watching someone you know died and you being one of the last to see her alive is always uncomfortable.

Especially when you know you could have avoided her death. It shouldn't have happened.

If The Voice intended to make them feel guilty, he certainly succeeded. The movie stopped without warning.

'As you see, this clip stops abruptly, just as Antje's life stopped abruptly. It was as if she suddenly went up in smoke. Because of you. And now you are going to experience the same. Thanks to you.'

A hiss sounded. Lander looked around, alarmed, as did the others.

Smoke crawled out from under a seat like a snake, slowly straightening itself up.

'Smoke, there's smoke. The carriage is on fire!' Karolien cried out and ran to the door that led to another train car.

She pulled, but it remained shut.

Lander followed her example.

They began to cough from the smoke.

With much effort, he managed to open the door so they could escape to the next car.

The boy and the motorcyclist followed them.

But the train conductor had picked the door closest to him to escape .

Of course, he couldn't.

The moment he realized that the other door offered no solution he ran to the other side, it was too late.

The other four were already in the next carriage, and the door that gave access to the next carriage had closed automatically.

They watched the train conductor agonizingly slow being consumed by the smoke.

They saw him go up in smoke.

Then the door between the carriages closed automatically and they could see nothing anymore.

Chapter 3

Train Wagon 3

'Help, please help us! Karolien started shouting and banging on the windows.

She was frantic.

Lander tried to calm her down, but that didn't work too well.

Until she gave up and buried herself in Lander's protective arms.

'We're all going to die, I'm afraid. As long as the emergency services or the teams from the NMBS don't come and free us, we are at the mercy of this madman. Just because we didn't pay attention to a girl a few years ago. Who could have expected that?' The motorcyclist moved his neck left and right as if doing stretching exercises. 'But that bastard has bullied us enough.' He took off one of his heavy boots. They had steel tips.

He banged it vigorously on the intercom.

He kept pounding on it until there were dents in the intercom.

Still not satisfied with the result, he took something out of his belt hidden under his t-shirt.

It was a knife. He began to fiddle with it on the intercom.

He used so much force that the intercom would probably not work anymore. 'There you go, if he wants to bully us any further, he'll have to do it another way.'

'What have you done now? Now we don't know what he's going to do?' The boy's face was flushed red. You could see the veins on his temples throbbing violently.

'We don't know what he's going to do anyway. If I must die, then not with games like this. Let him get angry and come up with something else to make our lives miserable. No more of this psychological terror. J'en ai marre!'

'This definitely won't improve the situation. He can kill us even faster now!' The boy with the hoodie shouted it as loud as he could to the motorcyclist.

'Then so be it, boy, better the short pain than the slow agony. I'm tired of leaving others behind and watching them die. 'No, let him press a button and blow up this train car. Good riddance.'

'Are you tired of living?' The boy tapped his finger against his head. Have you lost your marbles?'

'I could say the same about you!'

'Stop it! Stop it all! Shut up! It all became too much for Karolien.

It's that creep behind The Voice who is nuts. Now stop blaming each other. It doesn't do any good. It is Christmas Eve. A time of peace. Let's think about that even if we are in a hopeless situation. Christmas should be a celebration. It's bad enough that I'm sitting here with you all and may not live much longer. But then I still want to make it a party.'

'Karolien, you're right. Let's make it a party.' Lander thought it was a good idea.

Escape for a moment, however briefly, from reality.

'Too bad my backpack was left in the other carriage. I could have treated you to some cookies. Karolien sighed.

'I don't have anything with me either. I do feel like celebrating but Í cannot help you with that.' The biker sat down next to Karolien and patted her leg politely. Not in an offensive way but with a casual, amicable pat.

'But I still have my backpack with me!' The boy with the hoodie took his backpack off his back, 'I have something that belongs at a party.' The boy pulled a bottle of rum from the backpack, which he placed on the small table.

He also conjured up three joints that were carefully hidden in a small pouch in the lining of his backpack.

They were carefully placed on the small table next to the bottle of rum.

"Do you have another lighter? The biker was in the mood for a joint.

This was the way to spend your last moments.

'Sure, what do you think!' The boy rummaged in his backpack until he found his lighter.

The biker was already holding one of the three joints. 'Karolientje, you're going to smoke a joint too, aren't you?'

'No way, I don't do things like that.'

'Come on. There's nothing to stop you from having a go. You may only have an hour to live. What can happen?'

'You know what, you're right. What can happen to me? At least I'll have experienced that once in my life. For as long as it lasts. And you know what, I will do something else I feel like doing.'

Before Lander knew what was happening, Karolien kissed him passionately.

'Wow, Karolien, French kissing that guy, all bets are off, I would say.' The biker lit his joint.

'Hey, I'd like that too!' The guy with the hoodie took another joint and lit it up. 'Say aren't you through sucking face yet? I've got feelings too, you know.' The boy with the hoodie was envious. He wished he were in Lander's place. Maybe she'd become more willing if she'd smoked a joint.

Karolien stopped and took hold of the last joint. She held it in front of the lighter the boy was holding. The boy lit her joint. As a thank you, he received a smacking kiss on the cheek.

Lander was still dazed.

He was not easily startled, but this was something else. Imagine him meeting a girl who made his heart stop with excitement on a Christmas Eve.

Love at first sight.

Too bad they couldn't be alone here, or something more might happen this evening.

Now he had to accept the fact that he would never know what it felt like to make love to her.

'You want a puff too? Karolien offered him the joint.

'Why not?' Lander sucked greedily on the joint.

If only to forget the situation he was in for a moment.

But the peace was short-lived.

With a great racket, the door to the next carriage opened.

Again they heard The Voice echoing from the next carriage: 'Get over here. Now!'

'Go to hell!' The motorcyclist showed his middle finger to the empty wagon

'You have a choice: either you come, or it's over for you.'

'Karolien, what do you think? Shall we take a walk? I don't feel like exploding just yet. I'd rather enjoy you a little more.' Lander pulled Karolien upright.

She leaned on him rather heavily but stood up as well.

Together they strolled to the next carriage.

The biker and the boy just stayed put. 'Hey, loser, you're just a voice. You're nothing more than a voice. Who's to say you're not just a voice in my head, and that this isn't happening?' The biker continued to laugh. The joint gave him a happy daze.

'Who is that guy? Why does he want us to move again? Weird.' The boy was suspicious. 'Do you have something to do with this because seem very relaxed?' The boy turned to the biker.

'Me? I have nothing to do with this. Maybe The Voice is some-one who works for the NMBS, the Belgian railroad company?'

'But that's it: you're The Voice: NMBS or Natural Motorcyclist Bernard is The Voice.'

'Boy, you are losing it.' The motorcyclist's laughter began to get on the boy's nerves. 'Literally and figuratively, losing it, blowing, how funny.' The biker slapped his hand on the table with laughter.

'You're not normal, man. You're The Voice. You're him. I can hear you now while the intercom is broken: you're The Voice.' The boy flew at the motorcyclist and punched him in the face.

The biker's nose cracked.

'Ouch, you goddamn bastard, why are you doing that?' The motorcyclist, in turn, struck the boy's face with his fists.' You had it coming.'

A cracked eyebrow and a black eye were the outcome.

But the boy wasn't to let this go.

Both men began to fight.

They kept hitting and kicking at each other.

'Go ahead, beat each other to death. That's what I want.'

That comment from The Voice from the other carriage was enough to make the brawlers stop.

The voice's sound acted as a trigger start listening.

'I give you a choice: you will get 100.000 euros if you stay in this wagon and let the other person go to the next wagon, or you will both stay here to finish your fight. Just one problem: whoever remains here won't know what will happen. What's your choice?

The biker and the boy looked at each other. Their faces blemished with the effects of testosterone.

'100.000 euros?'

'But you don't know what will happen,' the biker said to the boy.

'I don't care. I'll take that risk. One hundred thousand euros, do you know what I have to do for that?' he said rubbing thumb and index finger together.

'I would think twice about that. I can do a lot with that money too, but you don't know what The Voice will do if you stay here. So far, the people who stayed behind in a wagon haven't had much luck.'

'Well then, I won't do it, but then we'll both stay here, then you can see for yourself what happens. The boy with the hoodie searched for his joint that had fallen during the fight. Would you prefer that?

'Uh, no.'

'Well, that's settled then,, right? Me the money, you can go to the lovebirds in the next carriage.'

'I wish you luck then. I'm afraid you'll need it.' The motor-cyclist hugged the boy.

The fight had been forgotten.

'At last, money, come to me!' The boy stood with his arms wide, waiting as if money would fall from heaven like manna. He took another puff from his joint.

The motorcyclist shook his head and hurried to the next carriage.

He shuffled a bit and occasionally had to hold on to a bar in the walkway.

The drugs had affected him more than than he thought.

The carriage door closed.

Chapter 4

Train Wagon 4

The motorcyclist came to Lander and Karolien, waiting hand in hand.

They heard a bang coming from the last wagon.

'What was that?

'It sounded like an explosion in the other wagon,' Lander said hesitantly.

'That was it, then. I'm afraid there are now only three of us left.'

'At least it went with a bang. That must have pleased that boy, Xavier,' the biker mumbled.

Karolien and Lander had left the joint behind.

For now, passion had also disappeared.

Who would feel like kissing or making love when people have just been killed?

But the silence didn't last as long as they would have liked because the intercom crackled again.

'Now it's just you three. A girl and a boy and a third wheel on the wagon.'

'What are you planning to do with us?' Lander said snippily.

'Such a sweet little couple. Such fresh love bliss. Too bad you won't be able to see it through. But then again, Antje couldn't experience young love either. Feel those butterflies in her stomach. Feeling the passion inside or knowing the pain of being separated. So it is a beautiful thing that you are in love. Now you will learn what it is like to have to miss a loved one knowing that you will never see your loved one again. Love hurts In the same way it hurts me that you neglected Antje, did not see her, did not listen to her. That neglect hurts me more than the hate I feel for you. The hate feels more comfortable than I thought. It is like a cloak that envelops me. It has been my companion since Antjes death. My loyal friend who keeps me going. I cherish the hate because what am I without it? What am I without feeling the pain you have caused us? What am I?'

'Are you Antje's father?'

It remained silent. Lander's question was relevant.

Most of all, he wanted to stall for time.

'Who I am is not important. What is important is who you are, what you have done.'

'What do you have in store for us?' The biker was beginning to regain some of his senses; it took more than a joint to knock him completely out of his wits.

'Time will tell.'

It became silent again.

No one felt like talking.

Karolien lay with her head on Lander's shoulder.

Lander stared outside at the snowflakes swirling peacefully down the air.

A peaceful, white Christmas.

The motorcyclist must have read his mind: 'The Miracle Club had memorable Christmas evenings. Everyone who didn't feel like a boring family dinner came there to party. The whole place was decorated. There was always a big Christmas tree at the disco bar. With glitter balls as baubles. Those were times. Unfortunately, The Miracle Club went out of business.'

'I would now give a lot of money to attend another one of those boring family parties. This was the first year that I decided to do my own thing and go on a trip to a Christmas market in the Ardennes on December 24 so that I had a good excuse not to be back in time for the family party. If only I hadn't done that, I wouldn't be sitting here.' Karolien sighed.

'But then you wouldn't have met me either. I'm glad I ran into you, whatever situation we're in now.' Lander kissed her on the cheek.

'You are right, Lander, about our meeting. I cannot regret it. If only it had happened in a different place and at a different time.'

The motorcyclist sat with his eyes closed.

He was still reeling from his joint.

Suddenly, he spoke: 'Say if The Voice is Antje's father, then he didn't do this alone, did he? There must be a whole group of people behind this, right? Maybe other relatives or friends of Antje's?'

'You're right, he really can't do this on his own. Even if he breaks in at night to put the cameras and microphones on the train, there were also television screens in the last carriage. You don't carry these around without being noticed, even on a deserted station.' Lander sat up straight.

'You have a point: the train conductor said that he does his round in the train every morning before it can leave. I can understand that he can't see those microphones and cameras hidden in the cars: they were minuscule, and we had to search. But the fact that the train conductor would not have seen that there were televisions installed in the last carriage seems strange to me. Surely he should have noticed that during his inspection?' The motorcyclist's brain seemed to work better because of the joint.

'Too bad we can't ask him anymore,' Karolien sighed.

'Unless those screens were put there later. For example, when the train had already stopped....'

'But Lander, that's not possible, is it? The Voice may. not always be there, but surely he has too little time to drag and install television screens?'

'When was he supposed to do that?'

'Bertrand, you're right: by the way, how would these screens have gotten here in this remote place? The Voice can't carry that alone.'

Lander knew they were right: The Voice was not working alone.

There were more captors.

Maybe they were outside watching them?

Lander realized that they had only been concerned with themselves.

They had lost sight of outside world.

The solution might lie there.

He decided to carefully study the landscape and placed his hands on the window, like two shields that were supposed to focus his sight on what was to be seen in the white snowy landscape that was only getting whiter because of the snow-flakes. Everything seemed so peaceful, so innocent, while here on this damned train, several people had already been killed.

And he might be next.

"What are you doing?

'Karolien, I'm looking if I see anyone. The accomplices of The Voice, you know.'

The biker took the other side of the train car to look outside. 'I see footsteps in the snow at the other carriage. You can hardly see them because fresh snow has already fallen over them, but look there, you can still see traces of footsteps!' The motorcyclist pointed in the direction near a rock.

Karolien and Lander seemed glued to the window.

'Good pick up, Bertrand! They are indeed footsteps. There are too many to be from one person.'

'So it's a group keeping us hostage. That definitely makes it impossible to escape.' Karolien said discouraged.

'Nothing is impossible!' The biker said it with the utmost conviction. 'I was a bouncer at The Miracle Club. All the things I experienced there. I've seen impossible things there. I tell you one thing and remember it for the rest of your life: miracles can happen.'

'The rest of our lives will be short, Bertrand.'

'Lander, you must never say that. Always assume the most optimistic outcome. We are too focused on the worst-case scenario. I don't mean that you should lose sight of everything and think that everything will just work itself out. No, be realistic and think positively. You never know what unexpected things will happen. Maybe we will find a way to escape after all. Someone who we can overpower may come in? I want to get out of here, and I will run.' The motorcyclist stood up and began to feel and push at everything once more to see if there wasn't something to loosen.

'Well, escape is not always easy.'

The Voice was back. 'Maybe even impossible. I must say your reasoning about me being ot alone, is interesting. Well, maybe your guilt is holding you hostage? Am I just the puppet who awakened your guilt?'

'Ah man, shut up.' The biker made a throwaway gesture.

'I have a challenge for you. Your togetherness is touching, by the way. Are you going to fight each other to escape, though? Let me tell you a story. A story about the underworld in ancient mythology. About Cerberus, the hellhound who guards the underworld so the dead cannot escape. Cerberus was a dog with multiple heads. In writings he usually has three, but there are also stories of over 50 heads. You might consider this train a symbol of the underworld because there are only dead people here: your "colleagues," and you are living dead. But you know what? I'm dead inside myself. Died when Antje died. So we are all dead. And we are guarded by Cerberus. Maybe I should let Cerberus go? What do you guys think?'

'Unleashing Cerberus, what do you mean by that?' Lander didn't understand any of it.

Until he heard the ferocious barking in the distance, he took Karolien's hand and pulled her upright. 'Get out of here!'

'Run, you two! If Cerberus has to be stopped, I will. I've never been afraid of a dog before, not even now. Bring it on, doggie! 'Come, doggie, come here!', the biker braced himself in the center aisle of the wagon.

Lander looked back once more.

The motorcyclist raised his thumb: 'always keep believing and keep on celebrating love.'

Lander ran with Karolien to the next carriage.

Behind them, they heard the ferocious barking of an attacking dog and the screams of the motorcyclist.

Then the door closed so they couldn't listen to it anymore.

Chapter 5

Train Wagon 5

'I don't want to anymore.' Karolien buried herself sobbing in Lander's arms.

'Everything will be all right.'

'That's not true, Lander. You know well enough that one of us two will be next in line.'

'Yes, I know,' said Lander threateningly.

Why did this have to happen to him now?

But he wasn't going to let it.

Not to him, not now.

There had to be a way to escape.

Lander detached himself from Karolien and began to look around very intently.

Nothing escaped his attention.

But no matter how concentrated he looked, he saw nothing.

He searched outside, but saw nothing that could help him get out.

Frustrated, he banged on a window.

The only effect was that he hurt the knuckles of his hand. Oh well, what was the point of it all?

How stupid could they be?

If only they had brought the lighter Xavier had with him.

They could have tried to start a fire, the captors would surely come.

They had been stupid to use it for lighting a smoke rather than to start a fire.

It was too late now to get worked up about it. They had been stupid.

Not looking for a way out more concentrated. When they had the lighter, there were still four of them.

Maybe that would have been enough to overpower the captors.

If, if, if ... It didn't do them any good. They had been stupid.

That was the only conclusion he could draw.

Now, all he could do was enjoy Karolien's company as long as they still had.

The Voice was back.

'Now there are two of you left. One boy and one girl. A king's wish, one would say, when it comes to children. But you are not my king's wish. I am just wondering: will it be the king who will survive this or the queen? Let's continue playing this chess game. I will give you one chance: either two of you will stay here, or one of you will go to the next carriage: which will it be: who will sacrifice yourself for your beloved, or will you remain lovers until death? But do you love each other if you would rather die together than give the other a chance to survive? A dilemma: what is true love: dying together or letting your precious live?

I would have liked the chance to philosophize about this with Antje, but I didn't have that chance. To lose your beloved is to lose yourself. For me anyway.'

'Then you are not Antje's father, but her lover or partner?'

Lander wanted to stall for the time more than anything right now. He wouldn't miss the opportunity if he could do that by asking The Voice out.

'Yes, I was her friend, her soulmate, companion, whatever you want to call it. But now she's gone. That is an unprecedented pain. I could just pick one of you right now or come up with a trial that would leave only one of you, but I won't. You will be given a choice I could not make: will you die together, or will you give each other a chance to live? Who will it be?'

'That's an impossible choice you're giving us. You know what: we both want to live!' Karolien shouted.

She wanted to live. She wanted to taste love.

She wanted to get away from this damn train.

She just wanted to be with Lander on Christmas Eve. Cozy together by a fireplace in a cabin in the Ardennes.

Just the two of them. But it looked like that wasn't going to happen.

'Oh well, inevitable and difficult choices are what life is all about, aren't they? We make choices every day, but what is the right one? A dilemma. That dilemma is what I want to give you as a Christmas present. To have to choose on Christmas Eve: how beautiful is that? A "Christmas dilemma". 'That's something different than a Christmas meal. What may I wish you for Christmas?'

'You don't mean that, do you? Just set us free, of course, what do you think! ' Karolien rolled her eyes.

'Ah, that's just one of the things I can't do. What about you, Lander?

Lander was silent. Was there an answer with which he could corner The Voice?

'That I could reverse my actions so Antje could return.'

'I can't give you that, but I appreciate you thinking about Antje. At least now I know you're sorry for what you did.' At that, The Voice became silent.

It was silent.

Could he have struck the right chord with The Voice?

Would The Voice give in now?

'It moves me that you will die feeling sorry for what you did to Antje. It is more fun to make someone die who knows why than someone who does not. Now I can proceed with peace of mind. But first, I'll give you time to decide: will you die together, or does one love the other so much that he will him the chance to go to the next carriage and perhaps survive? Think about it.'

The Voice was gone again.

'And now?' Karolien looked at Lander questioningly.

'Hmm, there must be another way out.'

'Lander, if you want to try to escape, I am okay staying behind so you can go to the next wagon.'

'Karolien, we won't. We'll get out of this together or go down together.'

They hugged each other.

'I know where we can hide, why didn't we think of that before! Come.'

Lander took Karolien in tow.

He could open the door to go to the partition where the toilet was. He entered the toilet with her.

'Stt, here, The Voice can't touch us here.' Lander kissed Karolien.

He knew this wasn't a permanent solution, but they were safe for now. Or so he hoped.

At least they would be buying time.

If The Voice wanted them to get out, he would have to come and get them.

The only problem: the typical smell of the train toilet. Unbearable.

Karolien gestured that the toilet smelled. Lander had to laugh. He had to restrain himself. He had no illusions.

The cameras must have recorded that they had fled into the toilet. They had to be quiet.

Lander felt in his pocket and grabbed his car keys. With these, he might be able to hurt or threaten someone who was coming to get them.

Far-fetched, but it was the only thing he could think of.

Lander listened carefully, ready to strike as soon as he heard someone open the door.

But nothing happened.

Nothing.

They couldn't sit here for hours either.

The smell had subsided. Or was it just their noses getting used to the stench?

Time passed agonizingly slowly. Lander got a cramp in his hand from holding his keys so tight.

A gurgle sounded in the toilet. What was that?

'Lander, the water in the toilet is rising!' Lander looked at the toilet, but the water was surging over the edge by now.

They were already ankle-deep in the dirty water. 'We have to get out. Open the door!'

With some difficulty, Karolien opened the door, causing a wave of water to pour into the hallway.

'Damn, I thought I'd finally found a way to escape. But then they had to let the toilet overflow: that's no coincidence. '

'Lander, I don't think we're out of the woods yet. Look! '

Water continued to pour out of the toilet.

Lander ran to the toilet to close the door, but it didn't work.

The water began to rise agonizingly slow in the wagon as well.

'They're pumping water into the wagon. Now what?' Karolien was frantic.

Lander tried to close the access door to the seating area of the wagon, but that didn't work either.

Neither the toilet door nor this door could be closed.

He started to feel at all the windows, but none of them gave way.

They were all jammed shut. So it was the entrance door to the other carriage.

The water was already up to his knees.

He pulled, pushed, even kicked at that door, but it remained closed. 'Damn, we're stuck.'

'We will die together.'

The moment Karolien said that, Lander was able to get the door slightly open Just enough to crawl through. 'Karolien, come.' Karolien waded in his direction.

Then The Voice echoed, 'The door will only let one person through. Decide what you want to do: die together or one person sacrifice.'

The water was already at their hips.

The open door did allow water to wash out, but it was too little; more water entered the train car than was let out.

The water that drained through the door simply remained in the intermediate section that provided the next train car access.

Lander turned around and wanted to go to Karolien. That was it, then.

But he had only just turned around when Karolien kissed him intimately.

Before he could recover from the surprise, she shoved him which made him fall against the wall.

She pushed him again when he wanted to wade back to her. He had to gasp for breath. He scrambled to his feet.

Karolien had closed the door herself.

She stood at the window watching him as the water slowly rose. Lander stood shouting at her, 'Karolien, no, what have you done? Open that door!'

She shook her head.

Karolien gestured for him to go to the next door that gave access to the next carriage because in the gap, too, water was seeping very slowly through the cracks of the door behind Karolien.

But with her, of course, the water rose much faster.

She kept frantically signaling for Lander to open the next door.

Lander didn't know what to do.

If he stayed here, he would die too, but he would see Karolien die first because the water was now at her neck.

Karolien threw him a kiss and looked at him with pleading eyes.

He had to go on to the next carriage. If only for her sake.

Karolien should not have sacrificed her life without purpose.

The whole situation was already so pointless. Lander pulled open the door to the next carriage.

He fell through the water that flowed forcefully from the wagon across the floor at the accordion walls that connected the train cars.

He got back on his feet and looked back one last time.

He saw that Karolien was entirely in the water now.

Underwater, she shaped a heart with her hands.

He did the same, stepped quickly to the other carriage, and closed the door.

He did not want to see her drown.

Chapter 6

Train Wagon 6

He sank onto the red train seat and cried.

'Bravo, Lander, Karolien must have liked you a lot that she sacrificed herself for you. But I understand your emotions. It's terrible when the one you love drowns. Like Antje drowned. The same as Karolien. Or no, wait: for Karolien, it was her own choice, not so for Antje, who was under the influence of GHB.'

'It was not Karolien's own choice: you forced her into it. You and your gang: you are guilty!' Lander shouted a few more curses at The Voice.

But he was shouting at a silent intercom.

It relieved him to yell and scream for a change.

After a while, he was through shouting. He had nothing left in him. He collapsed on the seat.

'Are you calm now?'

Lander had no desire to say anything at all. Whatever would happen, he would let it.

What would The Voice do to him now?

He didn't care anymore.

Not after he had just lost his new love, who might have been the love of his life. It felt like that to him anyway.

He felt like a robot. He was depressed and numb.

Meanwhile, the fear of death slowly crept up.

The fear first paralyzed his feet, gave cramps in his stomach, made his heart beat faster, squeezed his vocal cords, and numbed his head.

But when the fear of death had him completely in its grip, something unexpected happened.

Suddenly, confetti swirled down from the ceiling. Party music sounded. What the hell was that? Lander stood up in amazement.

It looked like a carnival. He saw some people standing outside around the train car.

They were jumping and cheering.

He coughed. Confetti had gotten into his mouth.

A door was opened.

A man in a fancy suit entered. 'Lander, congratulations, you are the winner of the game?'

'Game, what game?'

'Come outside with me, and it will become clear to you.'

Lander could not believe that he would be allowed to leave the train.

But the man beckoned him to follow him.

By now, he was outside. It was cold, not only in temperature but also in his heart.

Lander decided to follow slavishly. What else could he do? Perhaps it would offer the chance to escape.

A large circus tent was set up in the snow a little further on.

You could hear the sound of typical circus music and cheering people.

Was he dreaming? Was he hallucinating from that joint he had only taken a few puffs of?

What was this? Was it real or an illusion? Was he awake?

Everything seemed so unreal.

The man held open a curtain from the red and white circus tent and invited him into the circus.

Lander hesitated.

Would he even do that?

He could run away perfectly well now.

The man didn't look like a fast runner.

Lander first carefully spun around his axis to look around. He saw men dressed in black standing all around in the distance. They looked like guards from a security firm.

If he was to enter that tent, he would first take a good breath of the outside air.

It might be for the last time. He took a look back at the train.

There was nothing unusual to see.

It looked like an ordinary train that had just stopped in the snow.

He looked at the car in which Karolien lost her life. There was nothing to see.

No water behind the windows.

No, the train just seemed dry. Was this a dream after all? An illusion?

It was slowly getting dark.

Christmas Eve was approaching.

His family would be having aperitifs by now. He closed his eyes.

Deeply breathed the pure air donated by the trees once more and stepped into the circus tent.

Cheers sounded from the audience.

The tent was packed. He could not understand what they were shouting.

In the center of the circus ring stood an announcer. Smooth, hair combed back, dead straight.

Lander was pushed toward the center of the circus ring by the man behind him.

He hoped they weren't going to turn it into a spectacle like the gladiator fights in Rome?

A kind of modern bread and circuses?

That he would be finished off in the middle of that ring under the eye of an enthusiastic audience.

People had always loved this: the gladiator fights in Rome, the deaths by burning during the Inquisition, the guillotine during the French Revolution, and now the figurative killing on social media, the modern form of bread and circuses.

It wouldn't, would it?

'You've won The Great Illusion Show!' The presenter was jumping excitedly.

'The what? Lander no longer understood and was confused.

'Your family signed you up to participate in The Great Illusion Show. Doesn't that tell you anything? The presenter pointed out a separate box in the audience where his family sat. Hey, weren't they celebrating Christmas at the cottage after all? He saw that there were different boxes in which a group of people was sitting. Vaguely, Lander remembered a commercial on television a few months ago.

It was a call for a particular show that would air on Christmas Eve.

'But, but, then none of this was real?'

'Yep, it was real. You lived through it, right? The great illusion show follows people from the moment they get on this train and makes them believe in illusions.'

'Believing in illusions, what do you mean by that?'

'It's about the illusion you live in. You think you know the world, but you only know your world, not what is happening outside. You only know The Voice on the Train, what it tells you, and what you are experiencing in your train car, but not what is happening outside. What is real and what is not.'

'Yes, but what about that story about Antje? Did I ignore her like that, and that's why she committed suicide?'

'No, that story was made up by us. But the story does make it clear that you make choices every day that affect not only your life but also the lives of others. You never know what your choice will bring about in others. You can hurt others by your decision or, who knows, even get them killed. To what extent are you responsible for that? Do you remember what you are doing? What decisions are you making? The fact that you believed our story shows that we could make you believe anything.'

'So I didn't make her jump into the water?'

'No, Antje was made up by us. Fake. But you believed in it. Well done on our part, isn't it? It proves that we don't always reflect on our choices and sometimes even forget what we do or have done. Our brain often fails and remembers what is convenient for us. But we had you well down, didn't we? You believed it. Even the corpse in the suitcase, which was a doll with smell effects, was real to you. What does the audience think?'

The audience began clapping their hands and cheering.

Bread and circuses, people love bread and circuses, went through Lander's head.

'I must say that this was only possible with the cooperation of your family, friends, and work colleagues in getting you all together on this train. I must also thank the Belgian railroads for their willing cooperation. A round of applause for everyone!'

The audience meekly carried out what the announcer asked.

'And Karolien, where is Karolien?' That was the question that kept Lander busy.

'She is still alive. But what moving images, you have given us. The whole tent was crying. The viewers at home must have been moved too. Very beautiful. We never showed what happened to her. No, everything you thought happened was only formed in your head. It is your thoughts. It is your brain that made you believe that Karolien was dead. While she is very much alive, you will see her again soon. Your minds created this story, we didn't.'

Lander felt himself getting angry, furious even.

He could go off the deep end anytime now.

He looked at his family, who were just laughing and applauding. Just like the rest of the audience.

'Wave to the people back home too, Lander. Over a million people are watching this show. It's Christmas Eve. Let's be merry.' The man took him by his shoulders en turned him toward the camera.

Lander smiled sheepishly, which was in great contrast to how he felt and what he wanted to do: punch the man so that he fell into the dust of the circus floor with his shiny, smiling face.

But he couldn't do that in primetime on television, could he? Or could he?

He couldn't help but play along and act in this show. Holding up the illusion. The great illusion show.

'I haven't said what you won yet, Lander, because you are the big winner of this big show!'

'Where is Karolien?'

'People, the love is enormous. What do we say to that?' The audience cheered and went utterly wild. Lander felt his wet clothes sticking. He was cold. Literally and figuratively. He looked at the audience, stunned. Dis they all go completely insane?

'My dear Lander, soon you will see Karolien, but don't you want to know what you have won?'

'Oh, yes, I suppose?'

'First, let's report that 23% of the people at home voted for you as the contestant who would win this show. And from that, we will announce one person who will win the same as you!'

'People at home?'

'Yes, everything will be broadcast live. Do you know that you won a cash prize of no less than 100.000 euros and a worldwide trip!' The audience applauded. Lander blinked; a spotlight on him blinded him.

How he hated this. Had he been followed all this time by cameras broadcasting everything on television?

Had he been so blind that he hadn't noticed this? For a moment, he turned his head away from the blinding spotlight.

A girl came in with a sign on which the amount won was written.

A second girl came in with a colossal traveler's check so that Lander now stood squished between two walking large cardboard signs with slender legs.

'And how do you feel now?'

Lander wanted to say "miserable", but this was prime time Christmas Eve.

Could he?

Maybe he should just keep up the illusion, play the game, and put on a mask.

'A little confused.'

'I can believe that because what you've been through is something else. How did you feel when you thought you'd been taken hostage and your last hour had been struck?'

Couldn't that presenter just shut up and leave him alone?

But no, airtime had to be milked.

Broadcast time had to be filled.

Bread and circuses. Bread and circuses, Lander.

Perhaps there will also have been a big commercial break that made the television station a lot of money, Lander thought hoarsely.

'Not so good.'

'Folks, our Lander is still speechless from his adventure. Shall we reunite him with the other contestants? Shall we bring Lander back to reality or let him live in the illusion?' What do you think?'

The audience shouted for reunification: 'bring him back to reality, bring him back to reality....'

The audience roared what the show's warm-up man showed them on a large board.

'And here they are, the participants of our great illusion show: Wilfried, the man with the briefcase, our train conductor,

Xavier, our young guest who also won 100.000 euros, Bernard, the motorcyclist, and then of course ... Karolien, our Lander's brand new sweetheart!'

The main entrance to the circus tent opened, and everyone strolled into the arena.

His colleagues in the ordeal looked pretty good.

Xavier enjoyed himself and whipped up the audience, smiling broadly, waving his arms.

The older man had a slight smile on his face, but that might have been from looking at a specific box in the audience where perhaps his family sat. A young girl in her twenties waved enthusiastically at the older man, who looked exactly like her. The girl was a younger version of the older man.

The biker and the train conductor walked into the arena with their arms around each other's shoulders.

The last to enter the circus arena was Karolien.

She had a bathrobe on, her wet hair sticking to her face, but Lander couldn't care less.

Karolien was crying with happiness.

She came walking towards him.

The cheers of the crowd grew duller.

It faded into the background like a tune that played somewhere far away.

Love was the power that made it worth living.

Lander took Karolien in his arms and kissed her passionately.

This was no illusion.

True love was and is never an illusion.

The dull stuff

The Train
Taking the train on Christmas Eve is not always a good idea
Bo Vickery

Publisher's responsibility: self-published with the assistance of non-profit organization Cunamo, www.cunamo.be.
ISBN: 9789083128276
Legal deposit number Belgium: D/2022/14150/01
NUR code: 332
Cover design: Bo Vickery
Photo on back cover: Photography Paul Gheyle, www.paulgheyle.be

This is a fictional story. Any resemblance to events or persons is based solely and purely on coincidence.

This book has no chapters because a train is always riding, except the train in the book. And I want this book to be read at the speed of a train.

Inspiration and thanks

Inspiration for this book

As a child, I lived in a train station for many years. Even now, the train runs past the house where I live. My grandfather, father, and brother all worked for the Belgian railroads. For years I took the train to school in Bruges and to the university in Ghent. Hearing the voices from the loudspeakers daily in the garden made me think: I have to do something with that. In the meantime, I got tired of hearing the safety warnings about corona. That's why I decided to let a train play a part in the book.

Who wants to know more about the history of the Belgian railroads, I recommend the book by Gillieux Louis, The Belgian Railways. Yesterday, today, and tomorrow. Or a visit to the railroad museum, Trainworld in Schaerbeek, Belgium, www.trainworld.be

Also, my admiration for Agatha Christie, whose books I devoured as a child from the library of the Sisters of H. Kindsheid Jesu of my elementary school De Lisblomme, was an inspiration, especially the book Murder on the Orient Express for the location and the book And then there were none) for having the train passengers "killed" one by one.

In addition, The Train of Inertia by Belgian author Johan Daisne gave me the idea to write about a train.

But not only do books inspire a writer, but also music. The song The Train (De trein in dutch) by Sabien Tiels has always stuck in my head in recent years. About a grim, peeping tom and what you can get into your head.

The television show Sorry for Everything (Belgian television VRT) gave me the idea that travelers end up in an illusion. Just like the movie The Truman Show about a man who thinks he is living an ordinary life, but that is not the case. Those who have already seen this movie will understand why I mention this here. Those who have not seen the film should check it out if you want to know where I got my inspiration.

I wrote this book because I had promised my readers to release a book this year. But both the second part of the thriller series Nothing is what it seems (additional research needed in Bruges), and the children's book The Krummelingen (illustrations) are delayed (just like a train). So at the end of October 2021, I decided to write a book in 30 days. A short thriller.

Thank you

Finally, a word of thanks to those who made this book possible and helped with it: my mom, my brother Patrick who answered my questions about the railroads, my editor Frank Potters, who corrected my mistakes and made me see myself more clearly as an author, Frank also helped with the translation of this book, and proofreader Fabienne De Decker who sees errors and inconsistencies with a hawk's eye.

Want more?

You can buy my books on www.bovickery.eu/webshop

You can follow me at www.facebook.com/bovickery or www.instagram.com/bovickery13